Fifty Shades of Haiku

ELIZABETH CRANE STEPHENSON

authorHOUSE®

AuthorHouse™
1663 Liberty Drive
Bloomington, IN 47403
www.authorhouse.com
Phone: 1 (800) 839-8640

Published by AuthorHouse   10/05/2016

ISBN: 978-1-5246-2721-8 (sc)
ISBN: 978-1-5246-2720-1 (e)

Library of Congress Control Number: 2016914338

Print information available on the last page.

Any people depicted in stock imagery provided by Thinkstock are models, and such images are being used for illustrative purposes only. Certain stock imagery © Thinkstock.

This book is printed on acid-free paper.

His kiss was as rich
As a petal dipped is gold
My lips were in bloom

His soft fingertips
Feel like Egyptian cotton
Grazing my body

She smeared her lipstick
As she lustfully sucked him
Throughout the evening

The heat of his breath
Smelling of whiskey and sex
Enrapture our sheets

The steam of his kiss
Kindled the fire in my groin
So, I added wood

We rocked back and forth
Like a mattress on a sea
Swaying fervidly

Bending me over
He tied my hands behind me
Bound my mind with bliss

Sleeping next to you
Is like slipping in a glove
The fit is perfect

I touched his hardness
Like nothing to be crumbled
Laid inside my hand

I'm dehydrated
Wrung-out from sweaty passion
Give me all your cum

Like watercolors
Our sex makes soft, wet splashes
Of joyful color

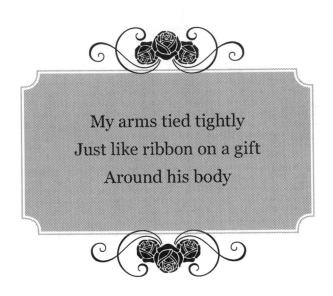

My arms tied tightly
Just like ribbon on a gift
Around his body

Dancing in the dark
His hands caress my body
My thighs heat the night

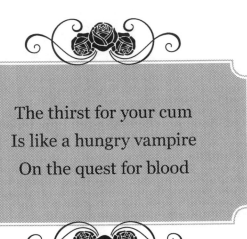

The thirst for your cum
Is like a hungry vampire
On the quest for blood

Twas the sweetest touch
His lips were like soft petals
Falling on my lips

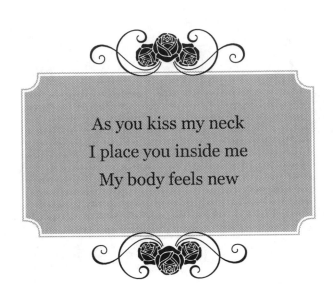

As you kiss my neck
I place you inside me
My body feels new

I want you to crash
Against my wet, thrusting waves
Get lost in my tides

Just like warm velvet
He slips into something snug
Something like myself

Dribbling in pearls
His bold paintbrush contoured lines
Alone he could color

With his fingertips
He decorated her breasts
Like leaves on a tree

Naked on my back
He sculpted my lean body
My legs opened wide

I scribbled his name
On his back with my hard nails
While the angels wept

He tickled her feet
With the French feather tickler
In her lingerie

In reverse cow-girl
Their bodies sang a language
Of their very own

Like a slip n slide
His body slid into mine
Wet from pink champagne

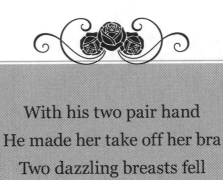

With his two pair hand
He made her take off her bra
Two dazzling breasts fell

She laid on her back
Euphoric from his warm hands
Rubbing her body

Our sex is fire-works
That explode out of passion
After a good show

The night that I came
For the first time in your arms
Tectonic plates moved

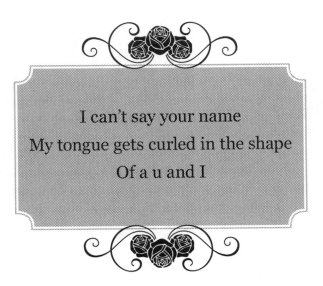

I can't say your name
My tongue gets curled in the shape
Of a u and I

Never have I felt

Such a darkness of a kiss

That the moon doth cry

With your sweltering eyes
You make my bed a campfire
That's been set to flames

To be nude with you
Is like the very first time
I still get nervous

My skin is sizzling
It's a slow burn for your love
Cool me with your meat

Like the flowing tides
Our bodies rush in and out
Again and again

If two is too stale
Let's add another person
Make wolves howl at night

Having sex with you
Is like flying to the moon
You take me to space

Such a violent kiss
That it nearly bruised her tongue
Black and blue by love

Like lightning he was
A hardness so electric
She felt ripped apart

Scratches down my back
As we howl like hungry lions
Starving for each other

My gut is starving
Hungry for the kind of salt
That comes in my mouth

His hands were like silk
Lightly blowing in the wind
Threading inside me

He drew a hot bath
Like sirens in blissful heat
Their sex made splashes

Their sex was music
Of two instruments colliding
Together as one

Rolling on the bed
Is like somersaults on fire
Put out by our sweat

They toasted Sancerre
Like two lover's applauding
For a game of love

Bouncing up and down
Like a frantic pogo ball
All over your love

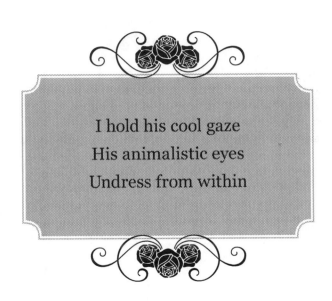

I hold his cool gaze
His animalistic eyes
Undress from within

Like leaves on a rose
My naked arms decorate
Your beautiful bloom

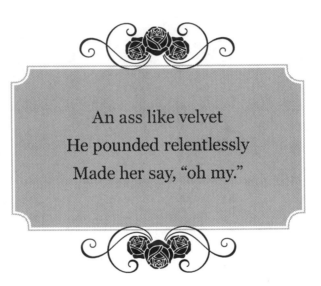

An ass like velvet
He pounded relentlessly
Made her say, "oh my."

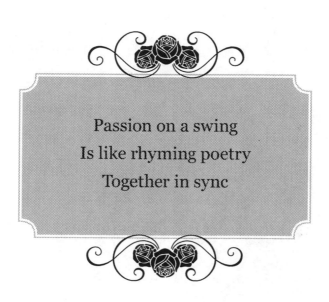

Passion on a swing
Is like rhyming poetry
Together in sync

Trembling with desire
My heated thighs are glowing
With fervor for love

Mimicking dancers
Their bodies gracefully moved
In each other's arms

Like bright white diamonds
Their bodies shined in the night
Two stars making love

A sound so alluring
Her moan so mellifluous
Angels danced in heels

My soul yearns with ache
As your agile hands touch me
Under the moonlight

His mind is like sex
The waves of his brain roll me
In eternal bliss

The blind-folding sash
Threaded around her lean wrists
Bound her to her chair

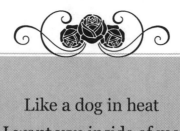

Like a dog in heat
I want you inside of me
Sex like animals

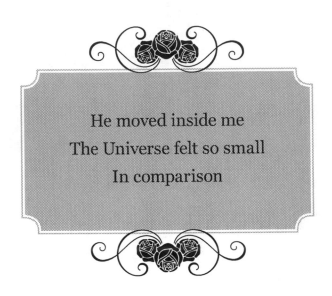

He moved inside me
The Universe felt so small
In comparison

On the pillowcase
He laid delicate petals
Our sex smelled of rose

In her lover's arms
She slowly rocked back and forth
On his hard manhood

He tied her lean wrists
Under her hot, steamy back
Wrapped in ecstasy

Underneath your clothes
Lies blissful hidden treasures
For me to adore

"Je t'aime," I whispered
As I nibbled his earlobe
While caressing his cheek

My thighs dripped in lust
At the mere thought of his touch
My panties were drenched

Our sex is in bloom
Petals looming in the wind
Caught by our desire

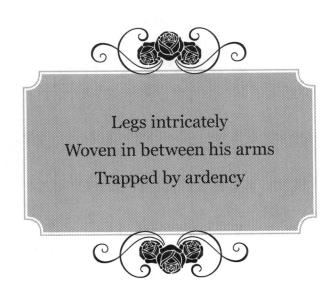

Legs intricately
Woven in between his arms
Trapped by ardency

She unzipped his pants
While binding him with panties
Victory was hers

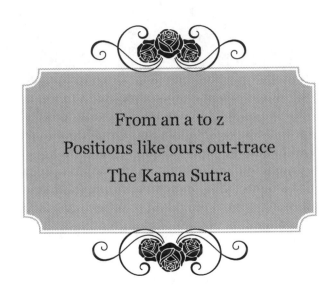

From an a to z
Positions like ours out-trace
The Kama Sutra

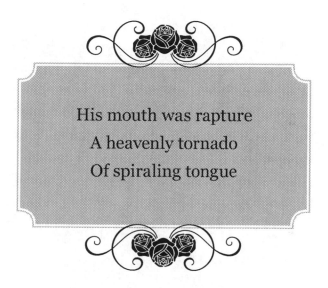

His mouth was rapture
A heavenly tornado
Of spiraling tongue

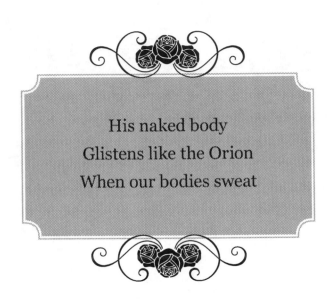

His naked body
Glistens like the Orion
When our bodies sweat

The scent of his skin
Is like sex in a bottle
It reeks of passion

He cascaded vodka
All over her large bosom
Suckled her breasts dry

Hugging you so tight
While you are inside of me
Feels like one body

He bit her lean thigh
Nibbled at her negligee
Lace tore in his mouth

A fit so compact
Is like struggling your manhood
Kegels may be thanked

He smiled softly
While I slowly undressed him
With my burning eyes

A flogger in hand
He whips me mercilessly
In this bed for two

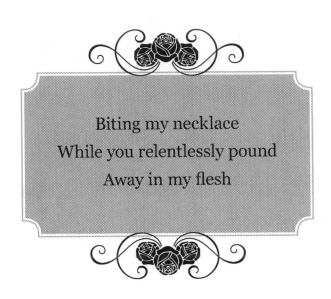

Biting my necklace
While you relentlessly pound
Away in my flesh

He grabbed her soft breasts
As he viciously pounded
In deep doggy-style

I straddle the chair
During this strip tease for two
Show you all of me

In white linen pants
My panties mimicked the hue
Of color beneath

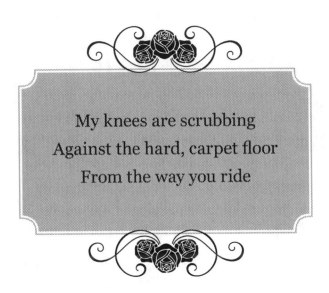

My knees are scrubbing
Against the hard, carpet floor
From the way you ride

For the last course meal
He drizzled her in whipped cream
Licked her for dessert

I have never felt
A size that tugs so deeply
It pulls at my heart

Sucking you is bliss
My tongue circling your manhood
Spins my tender heart

Scissor position
Cuts a part of my dark soul
Into shreds of two

Tangled in your arms
Is like being lost at sea
I cannot escape

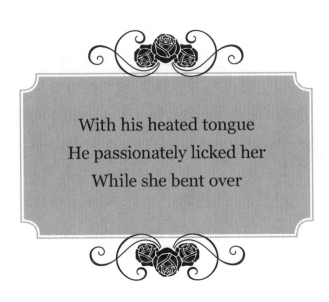

With his heated tongue
He passionately licked her
While she bent over

With my stilettos
My legs wrap around your head
Your mouth is dreamland

When you nibble me
My body starves for your soul
To complete my own

You drip words of lust
With your salivating tongue
I am wet for days

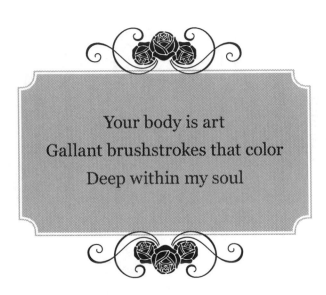

Your body is art
Gallant brushstrokes that color
Deep within my soul

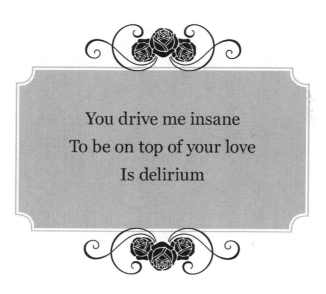

You drive me insane
To be on top of your love
Is delirium

Printed in the United States
By Bookmasters